PARANORMAL SEX COLLECTION VOLUME 3

EXPLICIT DIRTY EROTICA SHORT STORIES

BLAINE TELLER

plicit Press

CHAPTER 1

FLAMES OF DESIRE

IN DESIREE NYMAN'S OPINION, nothing in the world was as sweet as a good, long fuck with a couple of adventurous virgins. Sure, the more experienced ones sometimes had better techniques or more stamina, but over the last thousand years, Desiree found those things overrated. After all, one touch and she could make her partner hard again or channel back the energy to prolong the encounter. Enthusiasm was difficult to match.

College libraries were one of Desiree's favorite places to hunt. She never shied away from labeling what she was doing. She fed on her partners. Looking for them was hunting. She didn't physically feed on their blood or flesh, but enough of an energy drain could be just as deadly. Desiree had been around long enough that she didn't worry about that anymore. It had been a very long time since she'd lost control. She'd learned that keeping herself satiated was the perfect solution. And that meant fucking as often as possible.

Smokey gray eyes surveyed the quiet, nearly deserted stacks. Desiree tossed back a deep breath, scenting the air.

She could smell Pecans, a tang of smoke – both very male scents and so pure Desiree recognized only a few sexual encounters under their belt. She sniffed again and smiled. A pine forest with just a hint of rich earth. Another near virgin was close by.

It took her less than two minutes to find them and she instantly knew which was which. Pecan-colored hair and smoky blue eyes with a tall athlete's body. Desiree's sharp eyes saw his student ID. Everett Staples. He sat next beside a stack of European history books. On the other side of the table was a slightly older student, serious and studious. Thick raw umber hair and light blue eyes. Almost as tall as the younger one but with a firmer, leaner body.

Desiree licked her lips. They were perfect.

"Good evening," she pitched her voice low as she stepped forward, letting her power stretch out, caressing them both. She noted the immediate lust in their eyes at the sight of her lush curves. All she did was lower inhibitions. "Would you two like to fuck me?"

"Hell yes," Everett nearly knocked over his chair as he jumped to his feet.

Desiree suppressed a smile and glanced at the other young man. He didn't speak but took her outstretched hand. His name flashed into her mind. Jasen Raye. Anthropology undergrad.

She pressed herself against him, tilting her head up for a kiss. She felt Everett move behind her even as Jasen's lips brushed against hers. The electricity crackled between them, reaching behind her to wrap around Everett and draw him into their cocoon. Their clothing drifted to the floor with barely a glance, hands eagerly exploring newly-bared skin. Every question that threatened to disturb the mood was gently pushed away by Desiree. Instead, she coaxed their hidden desires, their fantasies, and fed her own wants back to them.

Jasen's lips slanted over her tongue, tentative at first as it traced the seam of her mouth. She met his tongue with her own, drawing him into the moist cavern of her mouth. His hands roamed her body, tapered fingers gliding across her collarbone, her full breasts. There, his hands met Everett's as they both explored. The younger man's lips trailed across her shoulders, his swelling cock nudging at Desiree's ass.

Her own hands were busy, knowledgeably tracing muscles, the logical part of her mind calculating what position would work best. She'd been wanting to do something – well, not new because she'd pretty much done everything in the *Kama Sutra* and then some – she hadn't done in a long time. These two were perfect. Both strong. The same height within an inch. And if what she felt was any indication, they were similar in more ways than one.

Desiree wrapped her arms around Jasen's neck, lifting herself up until he took the hint and helped. She didn't waste any time, hooking her legs around his waist. "Ready?"

Jasen nodded mutely. Desiree wiggled, centuries of practice working in her favor. She sighed as she sank down on him. A shiver ran through her and she let down her shields even more. She could feel Jasen inside her, but a part of her could feel what he felt. The warmth of her pussy, the way her nipples were hard bullet points against his chest.

. . .

"Everett," Desiree looked over her shoulder. His eyes widened as he read what she wanted on her face. She felt his shock ripple through him, followed quickly by desire. She fed back the latter.

"Please," Jasen spoke through gritted teeth.

Everett's hands were cool against her fevered skin. "Are you sure?" Desiree nodded, eager to move forward. She was hungry.

The initial penetration always had a bit of pain, just enough to add to the pleasure. Everett swore as he pushed the head past her rim and Desiree let herself reach into him, feeling the burn in her ass as much as the tight heat that gripped his shaft. She murmured encouragements as he eased forward, Jasen's voice low in her ear, swearing as the other man's movement rubbed against him through the thin wall of flesh separating their cocks.

She could feel them both trembling, struggling not to cum and she wrapped her energy around them, pushing her life force through both of them to give them both the control they needed. Everett groaned as he bottomed out, his balls coming to rest against her ass. Desiree rested her forehead against Jasen and felt Everett's cheek against the back of her neck. She let down her defenses, skillfully weaving the three of them together, the crackling energy surrounding them visible to her supernatural eyes. She was ready.

Everett's arms slid around her waist and the young men began to move, lifting her and moving in the kind of perfect rhythm that existed only with practice – or when a succubus was involved.

Desiree rode the pleasure, letting the men control the pace as they unknowingly drew the knowledge of what they were doing from Desiree's experience. Flames quickly licked across her nerves, muscles quivering under her skin, and the hunger uncoiled in her belly.

"Let go," Everett whispered, teeth scraping over her earlobe and she shattered, crying out as she

came.

Her muscles spasmed around her lovers and she felt their hips stutter. At first Jasen and then Everett emptied themselves inside her, and she fed, drinking deep from the sexual energy they released. Pure and fresh, with just the right edge to keep from being too sweet; her body shuddered as she came again, the pleasure of feeding washing over her.

When she stepped out of the library and into the warm summer night, she was sated and the young men were sleeping in their respective seats. They'd have a vague memory of her when they woke, but she'd be remembering that encounter for quite some time. She had at least a few weeks before she'd need to feed again.

CHAPTER 2

CURSED

TWENTY-YEAR-OLD PARAMORE WELDON had been doing this for a little over a year and she still hated it. She glanced at her watch. Fifteen minutes. Her light blue eyes scanned the diner. She'd lost track of time and now she was going to have to do something she really didn't want to. She pulled her long dark brown hair back from her face and twisted it up behind her head.

After eighteen months, she'd learned how to spot the best mark. There, in the corner, was exactly who she'd been looking for. Shaggy cocoa brown hair over an average-looking but brooding face. Sky blue eyes met hers, flicked away, and then came back again. A faint stain crept up his neck as Paramore made her way over to his booth.

"Hello," she slid across from him, legs sticking to the vinyl. "Hi," his eyes widened as they ran over her body.

She'd dressed for the city's summer heat: black short shorts that reached just below her ass and a bright blue camisole that hugged her curves.

"I'm Paramore."

. . .

"Sanders Eisenmann," he swallowed hard.

She got right to the point, all too aware of the minutes ticking away. "I need a fuck." Sanders jumped as Paramore ran her foot up his leg, letting her toes brush over his crotch before dropping her foot to put her sandal back on. "Up for it?"

"Hell yeah," he stammered.

Paramore moved back out of the booth. "Follow me in two minutes."

She didn't wait to see if he followed or if he was even watching. She'd see the slight widening of his pupils and heard the sharp intake of breath through his parted lips. He'd be there, probably in less than two minutes.

The moment he stepped through the door, she locked it behind him and grabbed the front of his shirt. "This way," she purred, pressing her body against his. Revulsion bubbled up inside her. Not for the young man whose lean, hard body was currently expressing just how willing he was to do what she asked. She was disgusted by what her jealous half-sister's jealousy was making her do.

Paramore didn't give Sanders a chance to do anything more but gape before she pulled him into the large stall. He sat down, hands scrambling at his waist as Paramore shim-mied out of her shorts. She ignored the squeak from Sanders at her lack of underwear and fished a condom from her pocket. She could almost hear the last minutes of her life counting down as she bent over the dark-haired young man.

She blocked out her surroundings, the fact that she was about to have sex on a toilet in some greasy diner's bathroom with a guy she'd just met, and focused on the half-hard cock in front of her. He groped at her breasts as she wrapped her hand around him. His fumbling was awkward, inexperienced, but his body responded almost instantly to her ministrations. One hand made its way down the front of her camisole and squeezed her breast.

As she rolled the condom over the young man's nicely curved six inches, she moved her legs to either side of his. Sanders removed his hand from her shirt, choosing instead to yank down the front of the garment, exposing both breasts to the air-conditioned room. His lips hungrily closed on the soft mound of flesh, teeth, and tongue worrying at it even as Paramore positioned herself over his hard length.

She took a moment to be thankful for his size – too small and she wouldn't get off fast enough, too big and she wouldn't be able to convert her pain to pleasure – and lowered herself onto his waiting member. She hissed as she maneuvered herself down onto his lap. She was always tight, that was a part of her curse, but now she was barely wet and the latex offered very little in the way of lubrication.

"Shit," Sanders swore, letting her breast fall from his mouth. His hands automatically went to her hips but he didn't try to control her movements.

Paramore ignored him. She had only a few minutes and the dry drag of his dick inside her was going to need some help if she was going to live. She began to ride him, bouncing herself up and down as she reached down to rub her clit. She closed her eyes, letting herself picture someone else beneath her, inside her. She couldn't see his face, didn't know what he looked like, only that their bodies fit together perfectly and they moved in sync. It was his voice uttering low oaths, his fingers flexing on her hips. It was his teeth scraping over her nipple, his fingers gently rolling her clit.

She felt it building then. The pressure she always dreaded and always craved. The jerk of Sanders's hips told her that he was close. She clenched her muscles and he came, an inarticulate cry spilling out of him even as he emptied himself into the condom. A slight tweak to her clit and her release washed over her, the accompanying relief almost as great. She was afraid to look at her watch, to see how close she'd cut it.

She rested for a moment, letting the burn in her legs subside enough for her to stand. As she got to her feet, she winced as he slipped from her pussy. She'd stayed dry enough that she was going to be sore.

"Thanks," she muttered as she yanked on her shorts and adjusted her shirt. She felt rather than saw his eyes on her, but she didn't look at him.

It wasn't personal. It never was. In a few minutes, he wouldn't even care. The encounter would've faded and Paramore would be halfway home, hoping her roommate had made dinner. After all, it wasn't like Sanders Eisenmann had been the one to break the curse. For that, Paramore would just have to keep waiting.

CHAPTER 3

DEMON FUCK

HER NAME WAS MORGANA, a dark queen floating in a dark and fiery world in the subterranean depths of the unsuspecting Earth. She had been there for millenniums, eras, coursing through the abyss with her dark wings and a pointy tail. Her humanoid body was strong and slender. She moved with the grace of a cat. Her eyes could stare effortlessly through the night, shining with yellowish orbs. Many a mortal that had the misfortune of coming to this world instantly shivered when they came upon her, as they did with many of the disturbing sights in this lair. At the same time, it was hard for any male, demon or human, to resist her charms.

The hellish environment was her kingdom. It had an unseen ruler and it had many lairs. But no one knew exactly how deep the place got, nor would they want to know. Jagged, mountainous rocks were at every corner and turn. Decrepit trees could be seen in some low valleys and ravines other than that, the place was nearly devoid of any resemblance to real nature. The cries and screams of the damned shouted and moved from every angle, invisible ghosts caught in the suffering of eternity.

Morgana smiled. She loved this world, loved her home, and was always horny. Sometimes, there would be another demon to fuck. Sometimes even a human was enticing enough to capture her fancy. She would grant that human being one moment to escape its suffering, to feel some pleasure in such a horrid and torturous place. Although she had many duties in hell, that was the one that gave her some sense of pleasure and even a feeling of humanitarianism. There was very little in her existence that made her feel that she was helping people, but sex was definitely a virtue to her.

This particular evening in hell, she saw him. He was chained from the feet, on one of the mountainous peaks. His sins must have not been too great, as he was merely chained and respectfully kept out of harm's way. In his loneliness, this man had resorted to extreme masturbation, rubbing his length up and down as it throbbed. The tool instantly captured Morgana's gaze. It was impressive and beautiful.

The man's head was bent back in pleasure, unsuspecting as his eyes were closed and he rubbed his cock. Morgana flew to the edge of the cliff to join him, slowly sliding between his legs and lifting his hand from his cock. , the man looked down and gasped at the demonic female who now accompanied him on his rock. His eyes widened and he trembled before feeling the woman place her mouth over his cock and start to suck him tenderly. After the shock slowly left his body, his widened gasping mouth slowly closed before opening again, this time producing moans and groans. She was moaning too.

The man's cock was already penetrating the woman's

throat. *God*, he thought to himself, *that feels so good*. He had only been in hell temporarily, though he had been pinning his mind to figure out exactly what he had done to deserve all of this. He had been a church boy, loyal and paying his tithes. Never had he gotten caught up in the pleasures of the world, though he had masturbated frequently and in the secrecy of his own home. He had heard a long time ago that masturbation was evil- maybe that was what had sent him here? Or it could have been all the times he secretly stared at women in the church. He was crying out for something or someone to save him, but maybe he would never get out. Now, with this demon woman between his legs, sucking him off, he couldn't help but feel like he was committing the ultimate sin. Maybe this sin would keep him here forever if he was not already banned to hell for an eternity.

His train of thought stopped. He couldn't concentrate on anything else. He moaned and groaned loudly, holding the demon's head and feeling her head go up and down. As he looked down, he could see her hair draped over his legs and her shoulders.

The woman moaned before looking up at the man's eyes. Her eyes were so powerful. They could convince him to do anything.

He was still erect and hard and the woman pulled her lips away from his cock. She had had enough sucking. She wanted to fuck, and she wanted to feel his hard and heavy cock in her pussy. She climbed up into his lap and shoved her pussy on top of his cock. The man was already moaning in pleasure. The demon shoved his face against her breasts, doing most of the work herself. Instantly, she was pumping her body on top of his, working his cock like she wanted to milk him. The man's head bent up like when he was masturbating earlier, but no masturbation had matched this.

Not even close. This was the first time he had ever had pussy. He thought he would overload from it all. That wet, coarse pussy held onto him so hard, gripping and spraying juices all over his lap.

As the woman fucked, her motions became faster and faster. The man felt shame as his fantasies were being answered in hell, getting the chance to fuck some wet and raw pussy. It felt so good, way better than he had even imagined. He was feeling like he might lose his cock in her. She was going to make him splatter cock juices all over her inner walls. It was too much to handle. His cock even hurt from her fast and relentless motions.

The man's eyes widened as he cackled nonsense, feeling his cum spew into the woman. Like a vial bottle, her could feel himself fill the woman up, giving her every ounce of cum he had stored in awkward repression.

As he breathed heavily in exhaustion, the woman's motions slowed to a stop. With strong hands, she grabbed the man's chin to look him deep in the eyes.

"I am Morgana," she said. With that, there was nothing left to say.

CHAPTER 4

DREAM-WALKER

A VAMPIRE'S TALE

ANDREW CHARLES HAD BEEN ROAMING the earth for three thousand years, trying to find his soul mate. At this point, he didn't care whether she was a vampire, human, or alien. He just wanted someone to love him. But it seemed like he just couldn't find the balance between being a vampire and a man searching for love. His hunger always got the best of him. Speaking of hunger, Andrew realized he was hungry again for the night. He would enjoy feeding again, after his talk with Damon, the leader of his clan.

The vampires in his neighborhood stuck together in various clans. Damon, the eldest of his clan, wore the crown of a clan leader. He offered advice to the other vampires, such as Andrew, suggesting that they feed whenever they were hungry. However, he never advised them to feed on innocent human beings. "Choose the scum of society, people who don't deserve to be alive," he always said to them.

. . .

As his eyes perused the place, Andrew tried to find someone to feed on. There was no one on the sidewalk; it was too early for pedestrians and this neighborhood didn't have hookers. Andrew extended his mind to the apartments around him, finding a single woman asleep in her bed. He materialized in her room, feeding leisurely, leaving her no worse for wear, with no memory of the experience.

After feeding on the somewhat innocent human being, grief and guilt struck Andrew. What had he done? If Damon found out he'd practically have his head. He decided from this day forth he would only dream walk; go into the dreams of these women and pleasure himself, without physically biting them. That way, nobody would get hurt. It was several days before Andrew found a suitable woman with whom to try dream walking. He'd met her at a grocery store. Andrew obviously didn't eat but he found strolling the aisles of stores often led him to find women. It was less chaotic than walking along the sidewalk, trying to find a new woman.

She was older than his usual choice, beautiful but strangely distant. "I'll get that for you, ma'am," he said. He helped her carry her groceries from the small supermarket to her quaint little apartment. She invited him in with no hesitation. Sex was lackluster and over before Andrew had even begun to enjoy himself. The overwhelming sense he got from this woman was crushing loneliness, the desire for companion-ship regardless of the companion. In this case, sex was used as bait for just having someone to go to sleep with rather than sleep alone. He left her that afternoon, deciding that he would return later while she slept.

As he slipped into the darkness of her room. She slept peacefully, like an angel almost. Andrew carefully examined every inch of her naked body spread delicately beneath the white sheets that she had wrapped herself in, as she slept. Andrew felt guilty entering this woman's dream. But he did, as soon as he sensed she was in a dream state. Her dream was bleak and cold; Andrew had the overwhelming desire to leave. But he found her and took control. He controlled her thoughts and brought her to a nice tropical vacation spot, next to the deep blue seas.

She was completely naked in her dream, like a beautiful goddess. He laid her on the sand and traced the length of her gorgeous body with his tongue. Working his way up to her inner thighs. When his tongue made contact with her moist delicious pussy, she let out an ecstatic cry of passion. Taking her clitoris into his hungry mouth, he sucked hard.

"Oh...." She moaned, closing her eyes and throwing her head back into the sand. His cock throbbed in anticipation of penetrating her moist heat. And as he darted his tongue in and out of her slit, he wanted nothing more than to penetrate her temple of delight with his huge erection. And he did, pulling his tongue out of her delicious pussy and replacing it with his long shaft.

· · ·

A soft moan escaped her lips as he penetrated her tender folds with his massive cock. She gripped onto him firmly as he buried himself to the hilt inside her wetness. Over and over, he penetrated her core. With his cock penetrating her insides, he leaned in and captured her lips with a hot passionate kiss. He was totally controlling every aspect of the dream. Strangely, he had no real desire to bite her; he actually wanted her to feel loved and appreciated, something he felt she had never experienced. She responded to his caresses, to his slow thrusting into her, passionately kissing him, arching against him as she came.

Almost as an afterthought, before he enjoyed his own orgasm, he bent to her neck, biting her gently, slowly sucking her blood. The taste of her on his tongue as he thrust into her was overwhelming. His cock pulsed as he shot his load into her, thrusting over and over into her pussy. She arched against him again, apparently experiencing the thrill of a second orgasm along with the apparent thrill of being bitten. He'd never thought a mortal could experience both, similar to what he experienced.

Andrew left her dream, finding himself in her bed, she sleeping peacefully beside him, apparently normal. He felt quite satisfied himself, both sexually and emotionally. The whole experience was rather baffling; he had never done something as selfless as he had done with this woman. The emotion he finally decided he felt was pity; pity that she felt so alone, for whatever reason.

. . .

Feeling no desire to wake up with this woman, whose name he had never even asked, he rose and dressed. As he watched her sleep, he entered her mind one final time. She was still dreaming, in her own dream this time, but in contrast to her original dream, this was more like the dream he had constructed for her. It was bright and full of energy. She was in the dream, apparently enjoying her surroundings. He found her and planted a single thought of love; that she loves herself. And then he left both her mind and her apartment.

CHAPTER 5

FORBIDDEN ATTRACTIONS

"I CAN'T BE SEEING you anymore Carmen."

"Why? What's wrong? Oh my God, you're seeing someone else, aren't you? And you're telling me this now... On my birthday. I can't believe this!" Tears welled up in her eyes. How could Adam be so cold? How could he do this to her? Her sadness and hurt soon turned into anger – then blood-boiling rage.

"It's not someone else, I promise...I – I can't really explain...You may not believe me." "You can't EXPLAIN. You selfish bastard. Get OUT!" Carmen bellowed pointing to the

door. She was still dressed in the sexy pink lingerie she'd gotten especially for the occasion. "Listen, it's not that I don't love you...We just can't be together." Adam tried to explain but

she was not having it. Her face was red with fury as she insisted that he tell her the truth. Why was he breaking up with her so suddenly?

"It's against the rules okay...That's why I have to leave, and we can't be together, anymore," he finally informed her.

"What rules, Adam? What rules? You better start talking or leave, right now."

Adam stood there, searching for the right words to say, this was the hardest thing he'd ever had to do, in all his entire existence. Why the hell did he allow himself to fall in love with this feisty young beauty? He could see that Carmen was hurting and she was coping with the news the best way she knew how, by lashing out at him.

She calmed down a little from her sobbing. "I thought you were different...I really did...I thought I meant something to you but obviously I was wrong. Now get out." She had a serious look of disgust, mixed with hurt and rage on her round face.

In that moment, Adam wished he could take away all this. It was never his intention to hurt her. But he loved her way too much to allow his selfish desires to be with her, leading to her ultimate demise. As he watched the tears stream down her cheeks, he hated himself. More importantly, he hated the situation that he was in. As a grim reaper, his only mission had been to collect her soul, but he'd deviated from that, allowing her a second chance at life. And now the forces of darkness had caught on to his doings and they had threatened to banish him forever in hell if he didn't end her life and claim her soul. However he'd chosen the latter option, and he'd come to say goodbye to her one last time before trading himself, in order to give her a second chance at life. A great sacrifice for the woman he'd fallen deeply in love with.

"I said get out Adam," she insisted pointing to the door again.

Adam decided to finally tell her the truth about everything. She shook her head, telling him that it wasn't true. But somewhere deep down in her heart she knew that

Adam would never lie to her. He told her about him being a grim reaper, and how he'd saved her life during her accident rather than claiming her soul. Her sobbing became louder and as Adam watched, his heart melted for her.

Wrapping his arm around her waist, he pulled her to him. His lips soon came crashing down on her with a hot wet passionate kiss that left her body squirming under his touch. Carmen purred as his lips left hers and trailed downwards to the nape of her neck. His tongue felt amazing on her tender flesh, and she beckoned for more of his sweet caresses.

Arching her back, she heaved her chest forward, as he skilfully found her bountiful breasts that had been held firmly together by her lace bra. Adam popped the bra straps off her shoulders and slipped her firmly round breasts free from the restrains of the fabric, taking her nipples into his wanton lips one by one.

"Oh Adam," she cooed raking her fingers through his soft silky hair. He always knew how to pleasure her. He continued sucking, licking, and teasing her twin peak, bringing about a great deal of pleasure upon her.

As he flicked his tongue over and around its hardness, tiny spasms rocked through her body, and her juices seemed to saturate the lace thong that she'd been wearing.

Carmen yelped when he slipped two of his long finger beneath the fabric of her underwear and into her warm core. Her pussy felt amazingly warm and inviting, and Adam couldn't resist the urge to fuck her right there on the wall in her living room.

Pulling the thong off her, he tossed the flimsy underwear to the corner of the room. Her hand was searching for his erection. The feel of her fingers gripping onto his shaft firm caused him to let out a soft groan.

Adam continued to caress her nipples as she stroked his manhood bringing it to the degree of hardness that she desired. "Now Adam now," she begged indicating her need for him inside her.

There was no hesitation on his part. Adam quickly yanked one of her long slender legs up, bracing it against his shoulders while he positioned his cock at the entrance of her slit. Her pussy was wet, and he stroked his cock slowly up and down her tender flesh, allowing her juices to coat his erection.

"Oh, God!" Carmen shrieked gripping unto his shoulders for support. His cock penetrated her core without warning. Her pussy shuddered as his massive shaft continued its hard upward thrust into her moist heat. Carmen felt the need to take him in fully and so she whispered it in his ears. He pushed harder, his cock penetrating deep into her temple of delight.

Carmen moaned out in ecstasy as he began thrusting his shaft upward into her wet pussy.

Each thrust was harder than the one before it, and before long, she could feel her climax approaching at an alarming rate.

Her moaning got even louder when Adam increased the momentum of his thrusting serving her with several long hard thrusts that left her pussy quivering. Carmen could feel her juices slowly trickling down her core unto his shaft. Griping unto his shoulders firmly she closed her eyes and almost lost herself in the sweet delicious sensations that coursed through her body.

A loud moan escaped her lips as Carmen summited to her earth-shattering climax. Her juices flowed out of her core onto his core, increasing his own arousal. Adam gave in to his desires and began thrusting harder into her wetness, letting out several loud ecstatic groans as he went along. Finally, with a loud, groan, and mighty thrust, he too peaked his amazing climax, shooting his load of cum into her warm core.

Slowly he slipped his cock out of her pussy, and his juices trickled down from her core, onto the floor.

Adam looked into her eyes and felt the love that she had for him. In that moment he decided that he would do whatever it took to be with her, regardless of the rules. The love that they shared was deep and internal, and worth fighting for.

CHAPTER 6

THE GRIM REAPER AND THE GIRL NEXT DOOR

THE NIGHT WAS DUMPING rain on the windshield faster than the wipers could keep up. Tim and Laura Stevens had been driving for 12 solid hours and the past 6 in a downpour that seemed like it had been following them relentlessly. Tim looked at his wife with eyes that wore exhaustion and reached over to put his hand on her thigh.

"We've got to find a place to stop baby," he said as he glanced over at her sitting there in her miniskirt and tank top. Laura smiled and reached down to take his hand and pull it between her legs. Her bare pussy felt like heaven compared to the insanity of driving through the deluge in his face from the rain.

"I'm ready when you are," Laura replied spreading her legs so her husband's fingers found themselves stuffed into the full bush that covered her pussy with coal-black hair. "What about those lights up ahead?" she asked straining to see through the windshield.

The lights turned out to be a small gas station with a motel tucked out around the back. Tim pulled up in front of the office and left the car running as he disappeared inside the small motel office. It seemed to Laura as if he was gone for an hour although it really was only about 15 minutes.

"Well that's done," Tim said as he climbed back into the car and Laura. "He about talked my head off for a while there, claims no one stops here anymore because of the ghosts. What a crock of shit!" Tim pulled the car in front of Room 4 and shut it off. "Let's get inside and out of this fucking rain!" he said to Laura and soon they were shutting the door behind them.

The room was clean and tiny but the beds looked damned inviting. Tim went into the shower while Laura laid down on the queen-sized bed, her legs spread wide and her black thatch leering at Tim. "Don't take long or I may not wait for you," Laura said with her fingers tracing the edges of her cunt lips buried in her thick bush.

Tim hurried into the shower and turned on the hot water. He stood there with the water pounding his back with liquid ecstasy. He was just getting used to the stream of water on the back of his neck when he could have sworn he heard Laura moan out on the bed. The second moan was louder. God she's horny, thought Tim as he soaped his thick cock with the small bar of soap. Soon he could hear Laura moaning constantly which only made him want out of the shower more. He shut off the water and made his way out into the room to see Laura lay back on the bed with her legs in the air, her hands grasping the covers of the bed tightly moaning like someone was eating her furry cunt. But there was no one there!

Tim watched as Laura wiggled her ass on the bed and humped against the air with her pussy, her rosy lips now spread wide open as they peered out of her dense snatch. Her nipples were harder than Tim could ever remember seeing them as she pumped her exposed cunt off the bed and pulled with both hands on the covers. Tim's cock now stood stiff and aching as he watched his wife on the bed. He reached down and grabbed his cock and began pumping his thick swollen meat in his big hand.

Laura's head began to rock back and forth wildly like it always did before she came. Tim's cockhead was coated with precum as he watched his wife thrashing on the bed while her moans got louder and more desperate. She's actually going to cum, thought Tim as Laura started to pant like she always did right before she squirted. The thought made him pump his thick cock even faster. Suddenly Laura gasped and shrieked as her hips came up off the bed and a splash of cunt juice gushed from her swollen cunt. Her hands had now pulled the covers to her sides, both hands. Tim quickly moved over to the foot of the motel bed, his cock swollen and angry, the head bulbous and dark red.

"Fuck, what's got into you?" Tim asked as Laura's eyes opened and she stared at him with a confused look on her face.

"I don't know," she replied as she looked down at her drenched cunt hair. "I was dozing off and all of a sudden it felt like you were eating me. I kept my eyes closed the whole time it felt so fucking good."

"Well it wasn't me," Tim replied glancing around the room suspiciously. "You looked like you were really into it."

"Just come here and fuck me with that fat hard-on you've got," Laura said as she got on her hands and knees and looked over her shoulder at Tim.

Tim moved behind her and pulled his huge cockhead up through her soaking wet lips. With a quick flip of his hips, he drove his tool balls deep in Laura's drenched cunt. She moaned out loud and buried her face into the pillow and started slamming back onto Tim's fat hard cock. She wiggled her ass side to side trying to drive his meat deeper into her greedy cunt. Tim reached down and grabbed his wife's hip with one hand while his other reached around and flicked her stiff clit. Laura's clit felt like a fingertip in between her long red swollen lips. He pressed on it firmly and then wiggled his finger side to side as he drove his boner deep into her wet cunt. Laura had reached beneath her and was pulling on her left nipple as her gasps and moans were muffled by the pillow.

Tim felt the first spasm in his balls as his cock filled Laura's cunt with thick hot cum. She shrieked again and Tim felt her cum soak his cock and balls with her orgasmic juice. As he kneeled there behind her and his cock started to shrink still inside her, suddenly the lights in the motel room went off. Then came a distinct hollow voice from somewhere in the darkness that neither Tim nor Laura would ever forget as long as they lived.

"You're welcome."

ABOUT THE AUTHOR

Blaine Teller is an emerging erotica author of many erotica kinks and sub-genres. Be sure to check out other books and leave a review if this story got you hot!

Visit my blog at Blaine Teller's Blog

Join my newsletter for the exclusive Blaine Teller's Newsletter

Sign up for Free Stories from Xplicit Press Authors

Xplicit Press Author Updates

Like Xplicit Press on Facebook

Follow Xplicit Press on Twitter

Readers: I want to expand a few of the stories to see where the characters can be explored further. If there are any of the stories that you would like to read more about again, I'd love to hear from you!

Keep In Touch
Blaine Teller
info@blaineteller.com